Bradbury Press

New York

The Old Ball
and the Sea

By WARREN GEBERT

Bradbury Press
An Affiliate of Macmillan, Inc.
866 Third Avenue, New York, N.Y. 10022
Collier Macmillan Canada, Inc.
Printed and bound in Japan
10 9 8 7 6 5 4 3 2 1

Library of Congress Cataloging-in-Publication Data
Gebert, Warren.
The old ball and the sea
Summary: A boy and his dog spend the day at the
beach building sand castles, watching ships, and
playing with the ball that washes ashore.
[1. Seashore—Fiction.   2. Dogs—Fiction]
I. Title.
PZ7.G2555O1   1988   [E]   87-15131
ISBN 0-02-735821-6

For Cathy
Thank you, Barbara Lalicki,
Mom and Dad, and Emily,
whose slice inspired me

BEACH →

12 MILES

Early one morning, Roy and
his dog, Buddy, were riding

to their favorite beach.

When they saw
the lookout tower

they knew they were
almost there.

Roy and Buddy ran
to the shore to watch
the crashing waves,

and to build a giant
sandcastle.

As they watched
a passing ship,

Roy and Buddy spotted
something bobbing
in the waves.

It was a lost ball,
smooth and round
and striped like candy.

The ball was unexpected—
a surprise from the sea.

Roy and Buddy spent
the whole day
playing with the old ball.

They ran all around,
kicking and throwing the ball

until the sun went down
and it was time to go.

Roy and Buddy went home tired,
but it was a good kind of tired.

They left the old ball behind
to wash back out to sea,
for others to find,
on another beach...
on another day.

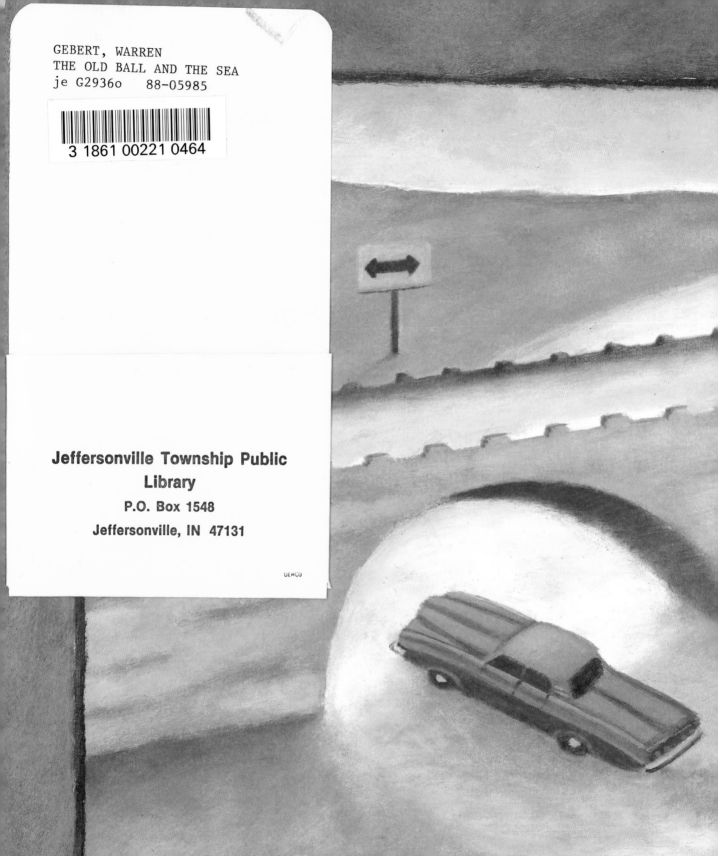